I0822859

# Chicatita and The Magic Stone

Elisa M. Olvera

Chicatita and The Magic Stone


ISBN: 978-1-61244-940-1
LCCN: 2020921590

Halo Publishing International, LLC
8000 W Interstate 10, Suite 600
San Antonio, Texas 78230
*www.halopublishing.com*

Printed and bound in the United States

This book is dedicated
to the students of
Main Street Middle School and
Our Lady of Solitude Catholic Church
in Soledad, California
for strengthening my faith
and Hispanic roots.

# CONTENTS

# SACRIFICING HELPFUL

## CHAPTER I

The sun was rising, a warm light washing over the bedroom walls. I could hear the roosters competing for the loudest *cock-a-doodle-doo.* It was time to get up, but the bed was so nice and warm. The thought of going outside to collect eggs early on a Saturday morning was right up there with going to the dentist-both yuck and dreadful. I just wanted to sleep. It was Saturday, after all! All my friends got to sleep in till noon. Well, at least that's what they said; they were probably just teasing me, knowing I had to get up and do chores.

As I peeked out the window, I could see the fog lingering just over the hillside. My thoughts drifted as I etched a happy face on the window, then gave it a frown. What was there to smile about, anyway?

Pablo had to get up early every day to check on the horses. How come he never complained? He was almost fifteen. I wondered how long he'd been on the feeding clock. I was a teenager after all. That was what teens did, right? We slept in. Actually, I would do it every day if I could get away with it. Why couldn't I get just one Saturday to sleep in?

"Uuuuh, okay, okay!" I said to myself. "I'm getting up!" I grabbed my pathetic, worn-out boots, and they barely fit anymore. At least my feet were growing, but what about the rest of me? I searched through a pile on the floor, hunting for my favorite hoodie and the rest of my work clothes. I fumbled over to the full-length mirror on the wall, rubbing my eyes open, and there I stood in my boots that forced my toes to curl. Shaking my hair loose, I pushed it away to the side, covering my face. Who wanted to see the other side of my face, anyway? They knew it was there. Then I muttered to myself, "Okay Chica, I guess you're ready to go. Whatever!"

Half-awake I staggered down the narrow hallway, the wooden floors creaking with each step. I could still hear the echo of Papá's footsteps when he would wake me before school to collect eggs. This morning I had just a few hens to collect from. Now that Papá was gone, the workload was too much for Mamá. My little hands held my balance while I adjusted in my boots. I missed him so much. His laughter still filled these walls.

I went down the stairs gingerly and gave my usual holler, "Mamá, Mamá, are you making breakfast? I don't smell anything! Where are you?" I could hear boxes and things shuffling around in the downstairs hall closet.

Mamá answered, "I'm over here cleaning out the closet. It's time to let go of your Papá's things. It is time, Mijita." Her heavy eyes glanced in my direction, and they had a sense of hollowness to them.

Standing at the door of the walk-in closet our eyes met. I began looking around as if I were searching for my right arm, but I was really just trying to ignore the obvious. My throat swelled up, and I could feel that familiar ache waking up inside again. "Oh, Mamá, how are we going to remember him? There will be nothing of him here." Then my insides couldn't hold back any longer. "Shit! It will all be gone, damn it! Gone! It has only been a month, that is not long enough. Can't we wait a little more? Damn it! I mean, really, aren't I entitled to a mourning period? You know, some time to grieve, Mamá, huh? This is BS! How can you be over it just like that?"

"Mija, first of all, watch your language. You know the rule! I know you're expressing yourself and feeling angry, but it takes time. You just take all the time you need, okay? You know, at some point we need to figure this out and keep going with our lives." Mamá put the box down and gave the hands-on-her-waist speech. "Do you think this is easy for me? Are you forgetting all those long nights I was up with your Papá? He was in pain and miserable, and I had to listen to him wanting to end it all. Did you forget all that? This is life, and it's just how it is right now, Mija. You know there are so many wonderful memories, and we still have this ranch. Papá built all of this with his own hands. How could we ever forget the sacrifices he made for us? So, together we need to find something good and strong to hold onto and get through all this. We may have to sacrifice a few things, but we'll get by okay."

Mamá's eyes followed me into the closet. She knew I was pretending I didn't hear a word she said as I carefully touched the sleeves of Papá's shirts. As if I were sniffing a rose, my nose met Papá's denim sleeve.

I sighed. "But the smell of him, Mamá... This shirt still has that musky cologne scent like Papá. It was his favorite. You can't just throw it out! You can't!"

Mamá's voiced softened as she said, "Well then, you keep that shirt. Keep it in your room, and when you miss him, hold it close and take it all in. You know that shirt may not have his scent forever, but at least you have his shirt. I know this is not going to be easy. I get it."

Mamá reached over, trying to comfort me, but I pulled away, angry tears beginning to roll down my face. It just wasn't fair, this life wasn't fair. I clinched my bare hands while standing up on my tippy toes, reaching for my memories off the hanger, and then I quickly ran back up-stairs to my room.

Entering the doorway, my watery eyes bounced around the room, looking for a special place to treasure Papá. I jumped on my bed, and I began shoving the memories inside my favorite laced pillow. My nose nuzzled into what was left of the lace stitching, and I inhaled everything. How could I forget all the laughter, morning panqueques, and even the time Papá yelled at me about dropping all the eggs on the kitchen floor. What a mess I made, but somehow, I got him to laugh about it with me.

"I love you, Papá," I whispered into my pillow. And then, with all I had inside, I screamed, burying my face into my favorite worn-out lace pillow and almost forgotten memories.

When I looked over at the dusty clock on the wall, I hoped it was wrong, as it said it was now nearly seven a.m. *Tick-tock, tick-tock,* it went, louder than ever. Oh no! I was late in chicken time. I had a job to do, and it wasn't going away, so I pulled up my boots by the straps, jumped up, and went floating down the stairs.

I wiped the tears from my eyes and forced the lump in my throat far down, deep enough to convince myself of this thought: *I may be small, but I'm smart and fast, and look at these muscles. I can do this!*

Waiving my arms in the air I walked through the kitchen and out the back door, slamming the screen door like I always did. Outside, the morning dew still left on the ground answered my tears with a new beginning as I tried to get through another day. I decided to meet my challenges con fuerza, grasping onto what I knew, which was being helpful-or as helpful as I could be-while making my way on this new journey called life.

# POWERFUL CHARISMATIC

CHAPTER II

My thoughts began to wonder as I kicked dirt and rocks on my way to the hen house, remembering the stories Papá would tell me. How I was born too early and was only five pounds. How I remained in the hospital for a month, hogging all the attention as I grew into a normal-sized baby. It was questionable if I would even survive. But I did, and Papá visited me every day in the hospital. He used to tell me about how I fought long and hard those first few weeks. How doctors couldn't believe my strength and powerful determination to live.

I liked the part of the story how they proudly named me María Lizette Ortega-Zapata.

I was named after both parents: María Ortega and Frank Zapata. And the name Lizette, came from my Tía Lizette Ortega, Mamá's sister from Texas. She was a Mexican healer, and we called her a curandera. I missed Tía, but I knew she would be here for Christmas to help with the tamales and to tell stories. I just loved her stories. In some ways I wanted to be just like her, charismatic and wise, knowing so many things about life.

She'd better come visit. Christmas was coming in a few days. "Damn it!" I said as I walked. "These boots are getting smaller, and everything else is too big. If Mamá heard me, she would give me a good one right now. Papá wouldn't have cared. He always said I should express myself. "Damn it, I miss you, Papá! Why did you have to leave us? Why? I could really just drop a Fbomb right now. A big one, Fffffuuh…"-My eyes glared up at the heavens as if Papá somehow knew just what to say. "Please, Papá, let me know you're near."

As I approached the fence, I could see left-over pieces of lettuce in the feeding bins. Carlos, our ranch hand, must have come early today for feeding, which was good. Now all I had to do was collect some eggs. We only had a few hens laying eggs right now, so Mamá had time to get a real job to pay the bills. So, I guess that meant going to the farmer's market on Thursdays and Saturdays. So much for sleeping in on Saturday mornings.

When it comes to breakfast, we always ate eggs, mostly because that was the easiest with the little egg-making machines so close to us. Living on a chicken ranch meant we could pretty much have eggs every day. We only needed to collect them. Mamá said there were so many things to make with eggs. So far, I had only seen scrambled eggs, fried eggs, boiled eggs, and something she called wrecked eggs, which kind of looked like a really messed up egg. What I really wanted to try was something called French toast, which she kept promising to make. She said it was kind of like panqueques with syrup. I was still waiting for the day she would make them.

As I began meandering around in the hen house checking boxes, I made sure not to cross paths with Big Boy. He was the meanest, most-bad ass rooster we had, and he would poke your eyes out! I wondered, where was that bad boy. I was still running late on fetching the eggs. Mom started calling from the house, wanting to get some eggs for breakfast. "María! María," She called. I wondered why she always did this. She knew I was out here, Chihuahua Mamá!

My favorite hen, Pío-Pío, was so precious and knew me as soon as I walked in the hen house or into the fenced yard. I loved how she came running over to me. She was so cute! "Where are you Pío-Pío?" I asked, making a kiss-kiss noise to call her.

There's a story with this little hen. When it was time to hatch, Pío-Pío had struggled to get out of her shell. But when she did, something wasn't quite right. She just lay there, so I pushed a little with my finger and she began to wiggle. For a while I kept her in a shoe box with heat lamps, making sure she lived, which took a few weeks. I felt like a hero. There was something pretty special about Pío-Pío, and now when I gave a *kiss-kiss,* she came right over to me, so I could pick her up.

"There you are Pío-Pío. How's my little girl? Are you making eggs? Let's see."

When I took a peek under her box, there was nothing there. I checked the other hens' boxes, and they all had four eggs. I wondered what was going on.

"What's the matter preciosa? Did something happen to your huevito machine, hmmm?" I ruffled her tail feathers, checking again. "You usually have eggs. We can't let this happen. You know what they'll do if you keep this up? It will be chicken soup for you. That's Mamá's rule, and we cannot let that happen! Tomorrow you better have some eggs under your butt!" I lifted her back feathers and blew on them as if that would help. "What the... Now come on, Pío-Pío. You know whatcha have to do!"

I got busy and began singing along with a Mexican Ranchera tune on the radio, which had probably been left on by one of the ranch hands. The familiar tune lifted my spirits a bit. I gave my best dance moves, and soon the egg cartons were full, completely filling the fridge for today's farmer's market. Maybe there would be enough to pay for gas and a new pair of boots. With all the wishful thoughts floating around in my head, I almost forgot the one egg carton for breakfast. Walking back out the gate I looked around to make sure I wouldn't cross paths with Big Boy. I began to mutter to myself as I walked back to the house. "I guess I'm gonna have to beg for that French toast thing. What should I bargain with? Hmmmm.

It has to be a good one this time!"

# AUTHORITATIVE WISE

## CHAPTER III

My eyes were heavy as I peeked out the truck window as Mamá drove us home from today's market. I glanced over at her and could see she was in deep thought, and by the worried look on her face, there were probably no wise men bringing gifts. Christmas would be here in just a few days, and she hadn't even mentioned a tree, presents, or if Tía was coming this week. By that look on her face I really didn't think there would be a tree this year. Things just weren't the same. There had to be a way I could fix this. What had I been thinking? I'd been so worried about Pío-Pío laying eggs, and here was Mamá with real stuff to worry about. She really looked exhausted, almost as if she were about to fall asleep.

I tapped on her leg. "Mamá, Mamá, wake up! Shhhhit, were you faking it? Aaaw, just like Papá used to do with one eye closed. That's not funny!

I thought you were gonna crash us, damn it! But you were just fooling around!"

Mamá changed to her serious, authoritative tone, saying, "Watch your language, young lady!" Mamá looked over at me quickly and couldn't help but laugh, so I busted up. Mamá leaned over and whispered, "Mija, everything is going to be okay. We are strong Ortegas and brave Zapatas. We will survive, we must remember our faith. God hears our prayers. We are not alone in this."

I interrupted, saying, "What kind of God takes my Papá away when I'm only thirteen years old, huh? Why? Tell me that, Mamá."

"Mijita, things happen in this world. It is not perfect. All we can do is our best, and we can remember to love one another, just as God loves us. We can keep our faith, which has gotten us this far. We must accept the life we have, but also remember that it is ours to make the best of it, Mijita. We must be grateful for blessings and not forget to hold onto our dreams." Mamá's grip tightened on the steering wheel. "I know the journey is unknown right now, but we have each other, and Papá is with us in spirit. Always remember, your memories are precious. Hold on to those. Talk to him. He hears you Mija." Mamá continued and seemed to be saying all this for herself to hear, too.

"Be strong and have faith. Ask the guardian angels to be with you each day. I'm here for you, too. Let's say a prayer and light a candle when we get home, okay?" Mamá reached over and grabbed my hand, giving it a squeeze. I could feel her pain, but she was trying to be strong and wise. Still, I wondered if she was strong enough for the both of us. I couldn't talk about it anymore. I didn't have the heart to tell her I didn't care about any candle or prayers. I thought to myself, *I'll just sit here quietly the rest of the way home.*

I began reminiscing about how Papá would stop for a cold strawberry paleta after we finished at farmer's market. I could see the paleteria up ahead. Mamá must have known I needed a paleta, especially today. We pulled up, and I looked over at her and whispered, "Gracias, Mamá. I love you." She forced a smile, but I could still see so many questions in her eyes.

I shoved opened the SUV door. "Race you, Mamá!" We shared some laughs and waited anxiously to get to our favorite flavors.

Mamá knew something was missing as we jumped back into the SUV. It had been months since we were last here with Papá, teasing and arguing over which flavor was the best to try. Yet there was some comfort in our paleteria routine.

Nobody could take that away from us. Not right now, anyway. Contentment filled my tummy after I enjoyed a frozen paleta. I couldn't fight drifting off; it was inevitable as we drove the country roads back home.

"Oh, Chicatita, wake up, Mijita. Look who's here." Mamá leaned over and tapped my leg as we drove up the dirt driveway.

I gently opened my eyes, peeking up out the SUV window. I wiped away the hair in my face so I could see the end of the driveway. I rubbed my eyes in disbelief. There stood Tía with a Christmas tree…if that's what you would call it. Poking out were a few uneven limbs, which were dangling, and there they both stood. But I thought to myself, *who cares what the tree looks like. We have a tree and Tía is here for Christmas!* "Oh, hell ya!" The words just came out. "Oops, sorry, Mamá. I'm just so excited!"

Mamá looked over at me with that look she gives when I have a potty mouth. Usually, she yells "caca mouth," but this time she couldn't help but smile at my excitement. After all, it had been missing for, like, forever. It was the first time in a long time that I came out from behind my hair with something to be happy about. Seeing Tía meant tamale making, cookie baking, and storytelling by the fire pit till way late while drinking Mexican hot chocolate. It was a tradition I looked forward to each year, and this year it meant even more.

Before we even came to a complete halt, I jumped out the SUV door, and ran over to Tía Lizette, yelling, "Tía, Tía!"

Tía reached out with one arm and lifted the tree with the other, "Chicatita, Mija, give your Tía a big hug. Look at you. I think you've grown!"

"No, I haven't, Tía. Look at me! I'm still wearing the same baggy clothes, but I think my feet are growing. Look, I need new boots." I stuck out my foot, shaking it around, and almost fell over. We both busted up, laughing. "But hey, I'm a straight-A student so I made honor role, and let's not forget the big cheese class president on campus this year! Not bad for a small chica. Uh huh, that's right!" After showing my best dance moves, I came to a quick stop and looked over at the tree balancing in her hand, "so, you bought a tree? It looks uh, a little... well, like it just needs some decorations. That might help cheer it up, ya think?"

We stood there looking at the tree in silence and then we looked at each other, then back at the tree again. Tía looked down at me, saying in her serious curandera way, "Well, when someone gives you something all you can say is thank you." Then we both looked at each other again and busted up with a good laugh.

I pulled on one of the pine needles, saying, "Thank you. It's the best Christmas tree ever!" What else could I say? She knew better, though. But who cared? We finally had a tree.

I looked back to see if Mamá was coming. In all the excitement I totally forgot about helping unload from the farmer's market. But that was the bargain I made. - If I helped unload and washed down the SUV, there was a good chance I would get new boots for Christmas. Just what every girl wanted… New boots so I could do more work on the ranch. Oh well. At least my Tía was finally here, and we had our Christmas tree.

In my strongest rancher's voice, I yelled over, "Okay Mamá, I'm coming! I know I promised!"

# EMOTIONAL IMAGINATIVE

## CHAPTER IV

The day was about done, Mamá and Tía were back in the house, chatting it up like they do. I had just about finished my chores, but there was still a dilemma tossing around in my head. How was I going to get my little hen to make more eggs? Well, I knew Pablo should be home now, back from his Mexico trip. There were only two more days till Christmas. I was sure he could help me come up with a plan. We both had imaginations that could fix just about anything. Hopefully, we could save Pío-Pío before Christmas dinner. How horrific it would be to have my own chicken as soup for Christmas dinner. I almost threw up at the thought of it. Yuck!

I decided to go back to the hen house to check again. Maybe she had laid an egg. My mind began to wonder, as it usually did when I kicked dirt clods. Pablo had been my bestie since first grade. We had shared some crazy, fun times, even when

I was getting on his last nerve. I began to realize how we'd been hanging out for a long time. It was easy. He lived just up the dirt road. We both hated catching the school bus every day. We still got along even though he made fun of me because I think too much, read too many books, use big words, and get good grades. He always made me laugh, even when he joked about my size. I always teased him right back, saying I couldn't help it if I was small. I would tell him, "Well, at least I have a brain that makes up for it!" I decided I would go see Pablo in the morning.

The sun was beginning to set, an orange glow covering the sky. It would be dark soon. Cautiously, I opened the gate to the fenced chicken area. "Pío-Pío, where are you? Now, where's that crazy vicious rooster? I know your hiding, waiting to poke my eyes out!" I crept in quietly, looking behind the gate and turning to shut the latch. Out of no-where Big Boy came out, went for my boots, pecking and flapping his wings furiously. I pulled away, kicking and screaming like a wild, bucking horse, being careful not to fall on my butt. Then for sure, Big Boy would peck me to death! All I could think was, *I don't wanna be that little girl at the ranch found pecked to death with no eyeballs and ugly boots.* "Aaaah! Oh my God! Get away Big Boy, Shhhh!" Giving a kick with my boot and making a swift turn, I managed to get away and run into the hen house, shutting the screen door as fast as I could behind me. Then I looked down at my boots. "What the hell! They looked like a cheese grater full of holes!" My balance came back, and I started looking for Pío-Pío. "There you are little girl. Now, let's see. Do you have any eggs yet? Damn it, no eggs! Okay, Pablo and I are going to come up with a plan to fix this no-egg business with you! See you tomorrow little girl, kiss-kiss."

I wondered why she wasn't laying any eggs. There had to be a reason. Just for a minute, I imagined what it would be like to be a hen. With my knees bent and my butt pushed out, I gave a wiggle, shaking and walking around in a circle. *How does an egg come out anyway? I wondered* "OMG!" I shouted. "Just look at me! I'm going butt nutty!"

I left the hen house shaking my head, then remembered to keep an eye out for Big Boy again. I went running to the side gate and closed it as fast as I could behind me. "Whew, I made it! Ugh! These boots hurt. Santa better bring me new ones now for sure! What a mess I am. Fuuuh… There I go again. I know, stop with the language, right, Papá?" I lifted my eyes to the sky, pulling back my long sagging bangs just enough to see Papá looking down at me from heaven. Then I giggled to myself. On my way back to the house, I had my fingers crossed. I was hoping to find some comfort food. It had been an emotional roller coaster of a day. I was especially hoping for freshly made, warm tortillas with Tía's fried frijoles and that delicious salsa. I thought I could smell something, and it smelled yummy!

# INTELLIGENT SECRETIVE

CHAPTER V

Sunset fell upon the Ortega-Zapata ranch. It was the night before Christmas Eve day. Our traditions had already begun with the making of sugary, cinnamon buñuelos and spicy Mexican hot chocolate, to be shared around the campfire while Tía Lizette shared stories that were sure to be haunting and spiritual. There was nothing like it, and I couldn't wait to get in my favorite campfire pillow-chair with a mug of hot chocolate dripping in whipped cream. There would be new memories made under a winter's star-filled sky, around a campfire that could blister the soul.

I cozied up by the fire, snuggled in my favorite blanket, and nibbled on the corners of cinnamon sweet buñuelos. "Okay, I'm ready!" I shouted. "-Come on! Hurry before the fire dies down!"

"We're here!" exclaimed Tía Lizette as she pulled up a chair. "Ahhh, this feels nice and warm. Mmmm, I love it!"

"Ya, Mijita, we're here now." Whispered Mamá in my ear. "Look at those stars! Amazing! Oh look, there goes a falling star! Quick, make a wish!"

"Why do people always say that?" I asked.

My Tía replied in her intellectual voice after taking a sip of chocolate, "Well, it gives people hope and promise that, just maybe, the stars will bring their heart's desires. Actually, it really isn't a star at all. They are pieces of rocks or particles that fall from the sky. People have been making these wishes for years, and why not just say it's a star? I mean, it looks like one, right?" I looked over at Tía wondering why I didn't know this stuff. It was basic science we learned in school. But now I was curious. "Go on, tell me more," I said.

"Alright, well, when we wish, many believe that our thoughts or deep desires go out into the universe and deliver what we're feeling. I once heard about a woman who wished for love after seeing a falling star and two weeks later, she met the love of her life. Then there was this other woman who wished for a way to fix her financial worries, and the next day she was offered a job when she was at the market. So why not wish upon a star. I say go for it! Maybe there's something more powerful out there waiting to know your heart's desires."

We all stopped for a minute and lifted our mugs. It got quiet except for the crackling fire. Tía continued, "But then again, there was that time we were all camping and Cousin Gilbert made a wish. He was so serious and secretive about it. Wouldn't even tell us what he wished for. Remember that?"

Mamá jumped in with, "Sure I do remember that trip. We were all sitting around the campfire, but the next morning he was all bent outta shape and upset. When we asked him what was wrong, he said, 'Those wishes were purro pethos and don't come true!' We asked what happened, remember? And he said, 'My wife zipped up her sleeping bag and didn't want to zip our sleeping bags together!' What a camping trip. We'll never forget that one."

My Tía laughed saying, "Oh my, I almost forgot that story. How funny that was. Cover your ears, María. It's grown up talk."

"Oh, come on, Tía, I know what you're talking about!" Mamá laughed so hard that she about fell out of her chair after that story!

My mind began to race, and I wondered if this was my answer to Pío-Pío's egg laying. I thought, *okay, quick, make a wish!* "Okay, I will!" I shouted out loud. I was pleased with myself as I made a wish. I should probably have thrown in a wish for a new pair of boots. I laughed to myself.

"You will what, María? And what's so funny?" Mamá asked.

"Oh, nothing, Mamá. It's a secret. Just making wishes. How many do we get, anyway?" I asked, hoping for no limit.

"The sky's the limit!" Tía shouted, looking up, "Really, look at all those wishes up there! Who wants more Mexican hot chocolate? That's what I wish for!" More laughs poured over the campfire, along with more hot chocolate.

I was beginning to feel the spirit of Christmas, or at least something that felt more like home again. A new kind of home. Different, but kind of good. I liked it.

# CAREFUL USEFUL

## CHAPTER VI

The day before Christmas had arrived, and the morning air was fresh and crisp. The sunshine woke me as it danced across the sheer window coverings. The anticipation of the day's festivities wrestled me out of bed. My thoughts raced from what was I going to do about Pío-Pío to how was I going to decorate that sad- looking little Christmas tree. I could hardly wait to run over to Pablo's house so I could see his funny face and what he brought back from his Mexico trip.

The morning was colder than usual, making the wooden floor cold to the touch. My dangling feet played tag off the side of the bed as I wondered what was for breakfast. Tía Lizette always had something delicious in the making when she visited. Then, with a push, I scampered to my feet and put on my-worn out fuzzy slippers ready to capture the day.

A cinnamon and vanilla sweet smell was billowing from the kitchen. It filled the air, along with my Tía's voice, singing over a Mexican song on the radio. I crept down the stairs, just enough to take it all in with a big whiff. *Could it be French toast? I wondered.*

"Tía, what is that you're making? It smells so yummy!"

"It is vanilla French toast with a secret ingredient I added just for you. After all, you are nearly fourteen in a few months. Isn't that right?"

"What secret ingredient does an almost fourteen-year-old girl need, huh? That's kinda weird, Tía. I just wanna try the French toast that I've been wanting for months and months now. Do I need to go get more eggs, or what?"

"No, I think I have enough here, Mija. The secret ingredient is for you to find true love when the time is right for you to blossom. You will know that time."

"Oh, Tía, that is ridiculous. I don't believe in that stuff. If it happens, it happens on its own time. You're always doing those special curandera prayers and stuff. Can't we just eat? I'm hungry. Is it ready yet?"

"Yup, have a seat there at the table. Hang on and I will bring it to you. I just need to add a prayer." Tía closed her eyes slightly and sprinkled the sugar and cinnamon all over the plate while whispering a prayer. Then her eyes opened. "Okay, there. Now it's ready. Eat it carefully. Here you go, Mijita!"

I gave a grin and slowly took a bite. "This is yummy. Does Mamá know you're doing this crazy stuff?" My fork lifted again and I said, "Mmmm, this is amazing, Tía, so damn good! You know she will flip if she finds out. Mamá is so protective of me. We will never hear the end of it!"

"Oh, no, I haven't said a thing. It's our little secret, okay? So, eat up and enjoy! How about some orange juice?"

"Okay, I guess it's our little secret then, but how will I know if it's true love, anyway?"

"Oh, you will know. It's a feeling you can't explain, and it will scare you and thrill you at the same time." Tía laughed and put the glass of orange juice down on the table, brushing away my bangs from my face. "And you won't want to hide behind your hair anymore. You will want to see the world with fresh eyes, breathing it all in. You'll want to feel it even though you can't explain it. Oh, you will know, Mijita!"

Tía Lizette always had a way of making me feel special and worried at the same time. I never knew what kind of special healing thing she was up to, but I was always curious, and most of the time it was her spiritual way of taking care of me. And I figured this true love thing couldn't hurt. After all, I would be fourteen soon. At some point I might even like boys more than chickens. I would maybe even have a Quinceañera. Some giggles overflowed as I ate my last piece of French toast. It was amazing, and I was content, my belly full. It made me remember Papá's words after we ate: "Panza llena, corazón contento."

I was ready to get myself together for a walk over to see Pablo. I had my fingers crossed that he might want to come over to help me decorate the sad-looking little tree with me.

As I headed upstairs to dress, I walked over to the tree in the living room and gave it one more long look. I wondered if we still had some lights that might work.

"Hey, Mamá, do we have Christmas lights and decorations anywhere? This tree really needs some help over here!" I asked out load while climbing the stairs.

I looked around for Mamá, wondering where she might be. Before I went into my room, I took a peek in Mamá's room. It was very quiet, maybe she's still asleep. All I saw was a motionless lump underneath the blankets. She must've been exhausted. Mamá never slept past seven a.m. I closed the door careful not to make a squeak and wake her.

I figured I would go see Pablo then, but I didn't know what to wear. I had the usual, baggy jeans and worn-out boots, which now had enough holes that I could hear little squishy noises of air when I stepped. I sure hoped Santa was bringing me some new clothes and boots. I tip toed down the squeaky wooden stairs with my squishy boots, heading for the back-screen door.

My Tía stopped me as I passed through the kitchen. "Mija, where are you heading off to this early?"

"Oh, I'm going to my friend's house to see how his trip to Mexico turned out. I will be back in an hour or so. Mamá is still asleep. She must be tired."

"Probably. We were up late chatting. I will save some French toast for her and put something special in it."

"Ya, well, no love potion prayers okay? We're not ready for that conversation yet. Is that what you all were chatting it up about last night? Men and all that crazy stuff? Well, ask her to find some

Christmas decorations so we can help that pobrecito tree cheer up or something. Okay laters, Tía!" I looked over at my Tía again, and she seemed like her cheerful self, but I could tell they had been up late last night. Her hair still had that messy look, and her eyes were heavy as she shuffled around in wrinkled pajamas, and it looked like she snagged Mamá's fuzzy slippers to wear. I couldn't help but wonder what they were sharing and what else they put in their hot chocolate after I went to bed.

So many thoughts continued to race in my head as I grabbed my floppy hat off the coat rack. I kicked the back-screen door, letting it slam behind me, still mumbling under my breath.

"She better not do any crazy-ass shit, that's all I have to say. Damn it! I know, Papá, watch the language. I'm not ready to replace you. I don't even wanna think about that!" I continued, muttering to myself as I went down the dirt road to Pablo's casita.

# SELF-SUFFICIENT ROMANTIC

## CHAPTER VII

The morning air was chilly, and the ground was covered in dew from the fog that had settled over night. California coastal winds were beginning to rustle what was left of the colored maple leaves. Winter was on its way. I squinted into the glare of the sun and wrapped myself tightly in a baggy denim jacket, then gave one last tug on my floppy hat. Thoughts continued to push through the corners of my mind. I was struggling to find a way to get Pio-Pio to lay an egg. There was a *whoosh-clunk-squish noise to my walk. I dragged my feet* against the dirt road, catching pebbles along the way. Then, all of a sudden, I kicked a stone so hard that it burned the front of my big toe.

"Ooow, shit! I hate these boots! Ugh! Wait… That's it! Ya, that's it! I will use a stone, a round, oval- shaped stone- and put it under Pio-Pio. She'll feel it and think it's an egg, and then she'll make more eggs, right? I can't wait to tell Pablo!"

The whitewashed gate was falling off its hinges, so I gave it a lift and a shove to get to the front walkway. It looked pretty dark and quiet inside. I wondered if anyone was home or awake, so I gave a ranch holler and knocked on the rickety screen door. "Pablo! Hey Pablo, are you there?" I heard footsteps heading toward the door. The front door opened slowly, and I could see a shadow behind the washed-out screen door. "Hey, is that you Pablo?"

"Hola, Chicatita, ya it's me. I just woke up. Hang on a minute," Pablo replied in a growly, scratchy voice.

My stomach was getting nervous. It had been almost two weeks since I had seen my bestie. I wondered if he looked the same or different. Maybe he had a golden tan from being in Mexico, or he might've gotten taller. Of course, everyone was taller than me. The anticipation was making my already curled-up toes squeeze tighter in my boots. The screen door slowly opened with a squeak, and there stood Pablo with a golden face and tossed warm brown hair that had been kissed by the sun. He wore washed-out hole-in-the-knee jeans and a baggy t-shirt that read, "Take me back to Yucatán so I can tán."

I just stood there, a little tongue-tied. He looked different, or was it me who felt different?

Then the words just fell out. "Don't you think you got enough suntán in Yucatán?" My sarcastic little voice, kind of cracked after reading his shirt. I was trying to resist, but I gazed up into his eyes, which seemed much more golden then before. Considering I was only using one eye, the other hiding behind my draping bangs, they were piercing enough to make me squirm in my boots.

"Chica, you always think you're so damn funny, don't you?" Pablo pushed open the screen door, then, with one big swoop, lifted me up over his shoulder, putting his boots on and grabbing his sweatshirt off the hat rack at the same time.

"Hey! My sunhat! Put me down! I'm not a sack of potatoes, you know." I wiggled around on Pablo's shoulders.

"Oh, it will be there when you get back, Chicatita!" Shouted back Pablo.

We exchanged the usual sarcasm. It was just like old times.

"Okay, you can put me down now, Pablo!" I demanded in a giggly little-girl voice. "Where are you taking me, anyway? I have something to tell you, and it's important. It's about my favorite hen

Pío-Pío. You know, the one I helped rescue." Pablo plopped me down like a heavy bale of hay, and I had to catch my balance. "So, are you going to listen or what?"

"Ya, of course, but I gotta go feed Pronto my horse. Come on. Follow me to the corral. I'm listening. What's up with Pío-Pío now?"

Quickly following behind, I began to explain my dilemma. "Well, she stopped laying eggs, and if it continues for a long time, she will become chicken soup. You know that's Mamá's rule, and I can't let that happen. I have an idea, but I need your help," I rattled on.

"Hmmm, well, what's your plan, girl? Maybe I can help. I dunno Chica."

"I'm thinking that if I find a rock or stone that resembles an egg and put it under her feathers,- you know, where the eggs come out- maybe she'll think it's an egg and lay more. Right? It might work, que no?"

"I don't know much about hens and eggs. I work with horses, but maybe there's a reason why she's not laying eggs. I guess your plan might work. Let's take Pronto down to the creek bottom and search for some stones that might work. I know there's lots of them there. You in for that?"

"Hmmm, okay, ya, but don't go too fast. Damn it! shit! I about fell off last time I got on that horse with you!"

"Oh, I see you still have a caca mouth, Chica," Pablo scolded.

"Hey, I'm working on it. Mamá doesn't like it. She says it's not lady-like and I need to find another way to express myself. I'm working on it, now, let's go then already. Hurry up!" I demanded as I watched Pablo toss a few shredded pieces of hay to Pronto.

"Alright, alright, let me get Pronto saddled up, and we'll head down to the creek, and this time hang on tight, so you don't fall off the back. You probably would just bounce like a rubber ball!" Pablo teased, laughing the proud laugh that always followed his pokes and jokes.

We finally got on Pronto and made our way with an easy trot down to the creek bed that sat behind the eucalyptus trees just down the dirt road. The thought of eucalyptus trees stirred up some memories, and I began to feel a knot ball-up in my stomach as Pablo went on and on about his trip. Something about Mayan sun signs, birthdays, and stone carvings. Who knew he cared about that stuff? Not me. Half of me was listening, and the other half was remembering the long afternoon talks with Papá under the eucalyptus trees. How could it be such a distant memory now? I felt guilty for almost forgetting. The memory shook me up, and I about lost my grip, so I grabbed the back of Pablo's leather belt. For some reason I couldn't help but notice how different he looked. His hair was longer, and his shoulders seemed stronger, like a man almost. Maybe I had never noticed before, or maybe something was different about a lot of things. My mind was doing somersaults. *Pull it together,* I thought. Finally, the creek was in sight and there were rocks-along the side of the dirt trail we were on. I felt myself staring at Pablo, so I quickly looked down and began my search for what I hoped was a perfect stone that looked like an egg. I poked Pablo in the back with one hand. "Hey, are you looking? I'm looking. Are you gonna stop or what?" I asked in earnest, ready to get off the damn horse. I giggled at my own thoughts.

"What's so funny back there?" asked Pablo. "Okay, this is a good spot. Now you get off the horse first. Remember how I showed you before?"

"Ya, ya, I know." I quickly glanced down at the stirrup so I could get a foot in. I could see a shiny green stone shimmering in the sunlight. "Look, look!" I shouted. "There!" I pointed down below the horse's hooves. "Move the horse up so I can get it!"

"Alright, alright." Pablo gave a *kiss-kiss,* and Pronto took a few steps back.

I jumped off the stirrup and picked up the stone. "This is it. This is the stone I need. Don't you think it will work?"

"I guess. Give it here. Let me see it!" Pablo acted like he was a stone expert. "Well, maybe or maybe not!" Pablo then gave the stone a big twenty-foot throw, and it landed in a dirty old barrel sitting out in the middle of nowhere.

"What the…!" I shouted at Pablo, catching my angry tongue just short of swearing a good one at him! I ran over to the barrel to get it out.

With my legs dangling up in the air, I screamed with excitement. "I found it! I found it!" I could hear my voice echoing in the barrel as I grasped the stone. My next yell from deep in the barrel was, "Help! Help! I'm stuck!"

Pablo laughing with a deep belly roar, enjoyed the predicament, watching with little interest in helping. He galloped over to the barrel and, using his horse for leverage, reached for one leg and pulled as he lunged back on Pronto, pulling the reigns.

"Back, back, back Pronto. That's it. Good boy!" shouted Pablo.

The force tipped the barrel over, rolling it on its side, and I came tumbling out with a high-pitched yelp, then scrambled to my feet. I didn't even take the time to notice the smelly, rancid eggs dripping from my jeans. Pablo continued to watch me scramble for words in all my excitement.

"You're really full of it!" Pablo said laughing.

"Well, maybe, but maybe it will work like magic!" I began to tip toe into the creek to rinse off.

"Maybe your hen will just poop an egg out!" shouted Pablo.

"Aaaah, this feels kinda good. It's not too cold. It's kinda refreshing." Certainly, Pablo could tell I was lying, but I continued, "So, then Pío-Pío would be saved from becoming chicken soup. Yup, that's right!

"Well, how does this feel, then!" Pablo snickered as he snuck up behind me, still on horseback, nudging me with Pronto's muzzle just enough to shove me into the creek.

"That is not funny!" I shrieked. We both began to laugh uncontrollably as I walked like a zombie coming out at the water's edge.

"Well, what's the matter? You cold, Chica?" Pablo asked, sounding smug. "Anyway, my rock is better."

"You have a stone? How did you get a stone? Was someone throwing rocks at you?" I teased.

"No, Chica, mira, I have it." Jumping from his saddle. Pablo grabbed his rolled-up brightly colored Mexican blanket, which had been nestled on the backside of Pronto. Reaching into his pocket ever so gently, he pulled out this amazing, perfectly-round, mossy, light green, spotted stone. It was oval and shaped like an actual egg. Even the size was very close to that of an egg. It glistened and sparkled when the sun hit it just right.

I couldn't believe my eyes. I walked over to him, my boots making a squishy sound as water gushed from the holes in my boots. But it didn't matter. I was mesmerized as I gazed at the shiny stone. Even Pronto gave a little whinny as he glanced over at Pablo's hand, which was lifted up into the heavens like he had won the winner's circle.

"Wow!" I said.

"Mira, now this is magical!" Pablo gave a wave over the rock like he was performing a magic show.

"So, can I have it or maybe borrow it?" I begged. "And are you gonna just hold that blanket? Is it your baby blanky, or what? Gonna make me beg for that, too?" I glared at Pablo.

"Alright, alright, I was getting it for you. Chicatita, your lips are turning blue!" Pablo's eyes met my lips. Nervously, he wrapped me in the blanket and quickly hid the stone back in his pocket. I felt a new warmth and comfort in Pablo's arms. A sigh left me as I snuggled up in the wool blanket.

I whispered, "Okay, okay, I promise. I won't lose it. Let's go then. Let me loose. I've got it. I can take care of myself. Let's see if the stone will work on Pío-Pío, come on. You got the stone, right?"

I saddled up with a lift from Pablo. I held on tight to the back of the saddle with an iron grip as we headed back to the chicken ranch.

"You got the magic stone?" I asked again while he settled back into the saddle.

"Yup, got it! Now hold on!"

Pablo shook his head, beginning to question what he had gotten himself into. He gave a *kiss-kiss, and* Pronto took off in a full gallop.

# KNOWLEDGEABLE CRUSADING

## CHAPTER VIII

A few hours had passed since I had left that morning. It was soon to be tamale-making time, and surely, they would be looking for me soon. Pronto pranced up the dirt driveway as if he were carrying precious cargo on his back. I could see Tía Lizette glancing out the front kitchen window, noticing the two of us on horseback. She gave an eyebrow-raising smile, probably wondering if this was her love spell at work.

When Pronto got to the gate, he was clever and used his muzzle to lift the latch, dropping us off just short of the fenced hen area. There, Pablo jumped off and tied Pronto to the leftover tree stump still in the ground from last winter. I quickly began to shed the blanket. I glared at Pablo wondering if I would get some help down. Considering my size, it was a long way to fall.

"Well, a little help would be nice cowboy!" I snapped.

"Sure thing. Just making sure Pronto is not gonna run off with you on his back, so chill, María. Your little hen is not going anywhere," replied Pablo.

My persistence was unbridled, Pablo was playing along, as he usually does. I could tell I was beginning to get on his last nerve. We came to an abrupt halt at the wired gate, and I said in a warning tone, "You see these boots?" I lifted my leg in the air, making sure Pablo had full view of my washed-out leather boots. "If you don't want this to be your boots or your eyeballs, watch out for Big Boy, a rooster with a fuuuh…" I caught myself and stopped short of swearing, and Pablo gave a glare. "I mean, with a flippin problem! He's mean and will peck your eyeballs out! So, ready? Now, open the gate slowly and make sure it's safe. Then we'll make a run for it to the hen house. Okay? Now open it slowly, slowly. Now, close the gate and run!" I took off like a wild colt. Pablo took a casual look around and sauntered in his cool, cowboy way, following me into the hen house as if nothing could faze him.

"So, you have the magic stone, right? You still have it, don't you?" I asked as we entered the doorway.

"I do, I do. It's right here, chihuahua Chica." Pablo pulled out the stone and lifted it just high enough for me to reach on my tippy toes.

"Now, Pablo, don't play your stupid games with me. This is not the time. I'm serious. Now, give it, please. Now!" I looked up from behind my bangs at Pablo, reaching out my hand in desperation.

"Alright, alright, chill out." Pablo handed the stone to me.

I brought the stone closer to my eyes and then kissed it for good luck. "Pío-Pío, there you are in your box. Alright now, here it goes!" I announced.

Placing the stone under Pío-Pío was easy. I looked over at Pablo, and I could tell by the look on his face that he was in disbelief and was about to give some smart remark. But he just looked over at me, and I looked over at him, then over at Pío-Pío, then back at him. Still nothing.

"Well, maybe it takes a while for her to feel it, Pío-Pío. Sí, se puede!" I proclaimed.

"Really, Chicatita? Let's go already, then. I gotta get home anyway and feed the rest of the horses. It's getting late, and my dad will get all over my cowboy ass!" Pablo exclaimed.

"Hey, caca mouth!" I teased.

"Hey, what? I'm almost fifteen. I can say cowboy ass, especially when it's me who's going to have to deal with my Papá!"

I looked over at Pío-Pío. "I wish you would just lay one egg. Just one. A pretty blue one, like the ones you used to do. Come on now," I Begged.

"This is ridiculous. I gotta go, Chica." Pablo headed for the door.

"Wait! Look, look!" My eyes lit up as Pío-Pío lifted up with discomfort. Out came an egg, then another! Then there were three! I looked up at Pablo with a sense of accomplishment and pride, but most of all I felt relief as we headed toward the door.

"Wait a minute. What did you just say?" I gasped.

Pablo turned to reply, "I didn't say anything. You're hearing things, girl!"

A high-pitched, thick, Chilean voice came from behind me. I turned back to look, and there was Pío-Pío sitting on a pile of eggs, flapping her wings in a panic. "María, María, wachu do to me here? Make it stop, ay. Dios mío! I was on my three months rest, ju know? I have a cycle for rest. I wasn't done yet! I'm an Ameraucana hen, chica, a descendant of Araucana chickens from Chile. This is too much work here for me, ju know, all at one time. I got blue eggs here, lotsa dem. Ay Dios Mío! Make it stop!" shrieked Pío-Pío.

I shouted, "What is going on? I'm so sorry, Pío-Pío. I didn't know you had a resting time. Nobody told me, oh no! How was I supposed to know that?"

"Why are you talking to the chicken, María?" Pablo shook his head.

"Don't you hear her talking?" I raised my hands in the air.

"No, I see some eggs, and a lot of wing flapping, and I hear loud cackling. It looks like a hen that's going crazy, and so are you, María! I gotta get outta here. This is too much, and I have horses to get after! Catch up with you later okay!" Pablo left, shaking his head.

"Wait Pablo, your stone! Hang on!" I reached down searching for the stone from under Pío-Pío.

"Ok, es todo Chica!" Pío-Pío gasped for air and fell off the pile of eggs onto the ground cackling. The hens were running for left-over lettuce scraps on the ground while eggs flew out from Pío-Pío's tail feathers like torpedoes, one after the other! "Make it stooooop!" squealed Pío-Pío.

As soon as I lifted the magic stone from under Pío-Pío's pile of eggs, the egg-laying stopped, and so did the talking. In a confused daze I wiped my eyes in disbelief and ran out the henhouse door, clutching on to the magic stone, leaving the freshly laid pile of eggs. My thoughts raced as I headed back to the house, trying to answer what had just happened. It was a strange and magical thing. Who was going to believe me? The back-screen door slammed behind me as I tried to find my breath after running as fast as I could. I knew just who to ask.

# THOUGHTFUL CONSERVATIVE

## CHAPTER IX

"Tía, Tía, where are you? I need your help!" Frantically, I searched downstairs. "Where are they?"

Up the stairs I went. It was quiet, too quiet. I tip-toed across the wooden floor and rested my ear on Mamá's bedroom door. I could hear muffled voices. I wondered what they were doing in there and if I should first knock? Or maybe they were in there wrapping presents. *I know. I'll pretend I don't know where they are.* I backed down the stairs a bit. I gave another holler. "Mamá, Tía, where are you?" I could hear footsteps coming toward the bedroom door.

It was Tía. "There you are. We were wondering what happened to you Mija. Are you okay?"

She must have sensed how frazzled I was, no doubt by the look on my face I was about to explode! "Tía, I really need to talk to you. It's important, but it has to be alone," I whispered into her ear, standing on my tiptoes. "Come on. Let's go in my room, okay?"

I grabbed Tía by the hand pulling her to my room. We had to jump over the maze of clothes tossed about the room. I tried to organize my thoughts. I pushed aside some clothes on the bed and said, "Let's sit. This is going to seem strange, maybe even crazy. I dunno, but I think you're the only one who might have the answers I need. I mean, you've seen some crazy shit, so here it goes…"

Tía gave me the "look.", "I know, I know. Language, right?" I sighed.

So there and then, across the lace throw pillows, I threw up emotionally, letting out all the feelings I'd been having all week about Papá, the guilt, and the anger. Tía listened carefully as I told her about all the weird butterflies I was feeling when I saw Pablo and how I didn't feel like that little girl who liked to annoy him anymore. I tried to explain how it was different, how there was something that made me feel alive, like I could breathe again. Then I hesitated, scared that Tía would think I was totally nuts when I got to the part about Pío-Pío and my plan about the magic stone. How I was the only one who heard a voice, and how I thought it was coming from Pío-Pío, with a strange accent and all. As I went on, Tía just sat there listening, with no judgment. She supported me, giving me a little nod of encouragement to continue on, and I did. It all came out like an opened soda can after you shake it, spewing from the depth of my soul. Then came a silence, so much silence that I could hear my heartbeat and the wind whistling through the trees outside my window, waiting to carry me someplace I'd never been before.

Tía's hand tried to brush away the hair across my face, but I pulled away. As if nothing had happened, Tía began giving me a lesson in spirituality. She told me that we are all spiritual beings having a human experience. She told me how our thoughts could become our human experiences. Maybe what I heard was Pío-Pío, or maybe I wanted to hear it because it gave me something to hold onto during a time of being emotionally fragile.

I was trying to keep up, grasping all that she was sharing. I mean, I'm no dummy. I've read a lot of books. But this stuff was pretty heavy to swallow. I kept listening, grabbing my lace pillow to squeeze on my lap. I could feel Papá's denim shirt between my fingertips, soothing me as I took in Tía's words of wisdom.

Then Tía said something profound. "If we want to heal our wounds, at some point we must stop reopening them and find peace inside our souls. There is something much greater than us that can help us all heal. I have seen the healing power of God through my work, and I have seen prayers answered. But there are also ugly forces of demons that lurk among us. Trust me, you don't want to go there! We make choices in our lives; we can choose love, or we can choose not to love. And that includes loving ourselves so that we can love others whole heartedly. We can rise like the sun each day, giving thanks for the light it brings us and with it each new day. Many choose to be angry each day, and they yell at the sun, hiding because it burns their faces." She paused and grabbed my hand. "You must live with these choices each day, María, deciding which road you wish to travel on. Practice your faith and cover yourself in a blanket of God three-fold. And always remember Mija, when you speak words, they have energy and power behind them. Those vulgar words, the hate language you use, will take you down, deeper into that black hole you're feeling right now. Are you with me so far? Is this making sense to you?"

I took a deep breath and nodded yes, even though I was perplexed. "What about the magic stone? Is it really magic?"

"Do you have this stone? Can I see it?" Tía asked.

"Yes, here it is." I pulled it from my baggy pockets.

"Hmmm, this is a jade stone. It's beautiful and vibrant. Where did you get it?"

"Well, Pablo gave it to me. He got it when he was in Mexico."

"Jade stone… well, it was found centuries ago and used in Mesoamerican cultures in the valley of Mexico. It was thought to be rare and very valuable for trading and making tools. Some people nowadays make jewelry with it. I have used it for its healing properties when I work on people, or even for myself during prayer or meditation. This stone has great color. It's wonderful, you must feel some sort of connection to it. It may be magical for you or something else.

At that moment something snapped in me. I suddenly snatched the stone from my Tía's hand, not letting her finish her words, and stood up. "I gotta go!" I shouted

"What? Where are you going? Are you okay, Mija?"

"Yes, I heard everything you said. I just need to give it some deep thought, you know. But I gotta run and make a wish. I'll be back before tamale making. Tell Mamá I went to the eucalyptus trees to talk to Papá. I gotta go!"

I ran out the bedroom door with a wrinkled denim shirt in one hand and my green magic stone in the other. *Click, clunk noises hit the wooden floors as I* raced down the stairs, flying through the screen door, slamming my discombobulated thoughts behind me. I ran as fast as I could, passing Pablo's house. I could see that he was out back with the horses, working, and didn't want to stop, not even for my floppy sunhat, so I gave a quick peace-out sign and kept on running. Pablo gave a shout out, but I didn't look back. I shoved the magic stone in my pocket, for fear Pablo would want it back. The trees were just ahead. The breeze was blowing, and the leaves shouted in my ears- words that were saying goodbye forever to Papá.

The warm sun was now shining on the side of my face. *The sun! The sun, I thought,* oh God, don't leave me now! How it burns! Tía's words rattled around in my head; the dark hole I had been trying to climb out of grew deeper, and the heaviness pounding on my heart with each step grew heavier.

I began my search as I grew closer to the forgotten tree. *I thought, where is it, where is it? I know the tree is somewhere here.* oh, there! There it is! Our tree. The tree that heard all the laughter and the tears that fell when Papá was running out of time. Here is where I will sit. Here in the sun where Papá can hear my wishes.

"I miss you, Papá. I know you're up there somewhere. I wish you were here for Christmas. I wish you could see me grow up and be proud of me when I win awards at school. I wish I could hear you laugh when I drop the eggs in the morning. I wish! I wish!" My tears began to fall. I was without words. The lump in my throat swelled up, and the flood began. Everything poured out from my insides, onto the memories we shared under this tree. I looked up into the heavens and shouted, "Papá, just let me know you're here. I just wanna feel you near me!"

I grasped tightly to the stone and pulled it from my pocket, then rolled Papá's denim shirt around my hand and planted my face in the sleeve, hoping I could smell what little there was left of him. The sleeve was now damp. I just sat there staring at the broken buttons, then wiped my drippy nose on it. Then, with a loud thud and a splat, something hit me on the head. It was wet, gooey, and warm.

"Eeeew, what the…!" I looked up at the sky, crying and laughing at the same time. "Okay, Papá, good one!" I wiped my hair to see what it was, and there was yellow yoke dripping from my hand. I wiped my hand on Papá's denim shirt, then looked up again and heard something. I couldn't quite see what was up there. But again, there it was. I heard that familiar high-pitched voice with a Chilean accent. "Chicatita, Mijita it's me! Up here!"

I rubbed my now-swollen eyes to try and see what it was, and there was Pío-Pío, flapping her wings and making little noises. "Pío-Pío, what are you doing up there? How did you get here? Can you even hear me?" *Okay, I thought, I'm talking to a chicken, I am going crazy.*

"I'm here for ju Chicatita. I heard you crying, so I came as fast as I could Mija, and by the way, my three months' rest is over now. As ju can see, the blue eggs are dropping!"

"Pío-Pío, come down here!" Then I gave a loud *kiss-kiss.*

I put my arms out and made a place for her to land, and she flew down. Her feathers were softer than ever, so warm and cuddly. "Oh, Pío-Pío I love you so much. No chicken soup for ju now!" I giggled.

"Ja, I know, but I won't last forever, ju know. Be strong, Chicatita. Have faith in a higher power.

It's real, ju know. And listen to your Tía. She's a wise woman, she gave me some words of wisdom, too, ju know. I like her!"

"Aww, so that's how you knew I was here. Pío-Pío, you're really something. I know ju won't last forever, and I will cry when that day comes. I will."

"I hear sumtin. Look Chicatita. Look who's coming!" Her feathers ruffled. I tried to wipe away my left-over tears. Suddenly, Pío-Pío jumped from my arms and flew away.

# CLEAVER PLAYFUL

## CHAPTER X

I frantically wiped my face and turned to see who was coming. Large, billowing clouds of dust were floating in the air, and the pounding sound of hooves galloping grew nearer. Oh no, it was Pablo. *Oh, chihuahua, I thought to myself, I must look horrible after all the crying and snot everywhere.* I tried to make myself look presentable, but all I could do was just sit there wiping my face on what was left of my denim memories. I felt drained and really didn't feel like explaining everything to Pablo. I hoped he wouldn't ask or notice anything was wrong.

Pronto suddenly appeared and came to a jolting stop, and a loud snort followed, probably because he had inhaled all that dust. Pablo jumped off as Pronto gave a good shake and one last snort.

"Hey, Chica are you okay? I saw you run by like crazy fast. Almost as fast as Pronto." Pablo chuckled, but he could tell I wasn't really into playing our usual games.

He knelt down close beside me but hesitated to talk. He wiped away a tear from melting the side of my face. "María, you're so beautiful." He then brushed away my hair, which I've been hiding behind for who knows how long.

I wondered if he noticed my smelly egg hair. My eyes were too scared to meet his. I was so nervous, and I didn't even know why I was even feeling these things. My head was tired of spinning, and my heart was galloping. *I thought to myself, Oh, dear God, please help me. Now more than ever.*

Pablo's voiced softened. "Everything is going to be alright. You'll see. I know it's not easy, María. Don't hide anymore. I wanna see your smile again, like when we were kids. Remember how we used to laugh and play down here at the creek? Oh, and I have something that might put a smile on your face," Pablo teased.

Like a proud, gallant knight in shining armor, Pablo strutted over to Pronto's saddle bags and pulled out a paper bag with something in it. Pablo handed it to me and knelt back down beside me. "Open it. It's for you."

The bag was heavy. "What is it?" I asked.

"You'll see! Just open it!"

The paper bag was crinkled and worn out, like it had been hiding somewhere for years. I opened it and felt something hard inside. I reached in and pulled out a brand-new leather boot. It was beautiful and rusty brown, with gold stitching across the top of it. On the side was more gold stitching, along with jewels that sparkled in the sunlight. He was right. I couldn't help but smile. I didn't know what to say. I was shocked and happy at the same time.

"Pablo, it's beautiful! How did you know? I mean, how did you know I needed new boots?"

"Well, I figured your foot would grow eventually, so I bought 'em when I was in Mexico. I took a guess on the size, so I hope they fit. You know, there are two in the bag. Get it out and try 'em both on Chica."

Pablo seemed eager for me to put them on. He then whispered, "But before you do, take the other boot outta the bag and turn it upside down. Then put your hand under it, okay?"

"Okay, I guess," I replied hesitantly.

The boots still had that fresh leather smell I loved when they were new. I didn't want to scratch them, so I carefully turned it upside down grabbing it by the heel of the boot and putting my other hand beneath it. Slowly, I turned it, wondering what might be inside. I could hear something sliding around in there, and a warm, shiny, green, flat, small round stone fell out into my hand. I looked closer, and it had some kind of sign engraved on it, a symbol of some sort. Then my mouth was left open as I gasped for air, watching it shine in the palm of my hand. It was tied to a thin leather strap.

"Pablo!" I shouted, "It's beautiful!"

I sat there not really sure what to do with it. Pablo looked at me, noticing I wasn't quite sure what to do.

"You wear it on your neck like this."

Pablo put the leather strap around my neck, then pretended to choke me. We both laughed. He could tell I was nervous, especially now that he had pulled my hair away from my face, I felt like he could see all of me now. No more hiding.

He then let go of the leather necklace. Pulling my hair away from my face. he leaned in and kissed me on the cheek ever so gently, saying, "Merry Christmas, María. I love you, Preciosa."

It was too unexpected, and I felt my spirits being lifted. "Thank you," I replied. I felt his warmth and sincerity. "Merry Christmas, Pablo.

I love you, too, bestie." Then I kicked him in the knee with my new boot. Pablo jumped up. "Hey, so you think you're tough now, huh? Well, put 'em on. Let's go! Tamales are waiting!"

"I hope so. I'm ready! Oh, and you should see the Christmas tree. Pobrecito tree needs help. You can help beguile the time while decorating, okay tough guy?"

"There you go again with the big words," Pablo teased.

"Get used to it cowboy, or are you just going to stand there looking bewildered?" I looked down at the pendant now laying on my skin. "And what is this symbol carved on the stone? Is it a magic spell or what?"

Pablo explained, "No, crazy girl, are you still all caught up in magic stone stuff? That is a Mayan sun sign for your birth date at the end of March. It means clever and playful. That's you, isn't it?" Pablo took a step closer and carefully lifted the pendant. It took my breath away. I could feel his warm hand. "Did you already forget the story I told you about the Mayans and the calendars? Remember that story?"

I jumped back, feeling a bit nervous, saying, "Ya, cowboy, I remember."

I looked up in his eyes. He could tell I was giving him pethos- you know, lies. So, I quickly shouted, "Ya, that's me alight, clever and playful, all rolled into one smart Chica. So, let the Mayan sunshine fall down on me. I'm ready for it!"

Pablo grabbed a boot and lifted it up to the sun, watching the jewels glisten. They were almost too fancy to wear, but I couldn't wait to try them on. They were just so beautiful. My dusty, worn-out, old boots came off with ease. My toes were still numb from being damp and squished. The bejeweled new boot slid right on, with room for my toes to wiggle, and it felt good. It was a perfect fit. Now I was ready to go. I got both boots on after coaxing the other boot away from Pablo, and my baggy jeans slid right over them. My eyes caught Pablo's eyes as he watched me stomp around in my new boots and Papá's shirt wrapped around my waist. He laughed, and I smiled back with a face now full of less darkness. "Thank you," I mouthed back at him. I picked up my old boots and waddled back over to a spot underneath the eucalyptus tree, leaving them there.

I looked down at my new boots, the shiny, green, jade stone-reminding me how clever and playful I really was, and just then I remembered Tía Lizette's words. "Wishes do come true, in their own time and place." I looked up into the heavens and said thank you to our God, full of new faith that was bigger and greater than ever before. It was there with the warmth of the sun on my face. I chose to feel the light of God and began to let go of the pain, and then I turned around to see what a wonderful friend I had. I gave him a smile.

"You ready to get up on Pronto?" Pablo lifted me up and put me up front on the saddle.

"Say what?" I shouted. Then Pablo jumped on the back of the saddle. Pronto gave a loud whinny, probably protesting the weight on his backside.

Pablo teased, "It's about time you learn how to ride Chica!"

We laughed so hard, and I almost fell of the saddle because my boots were nowhere near the stirrups, but somehow, I felt safe. Safe with Pablo's strong arms around me, helping hold the reigns while Pronto took us back to the ranch in an Andalusian fancy prance. It was finally tamale-making time and Christmas Eve felt like it had never felt before.

Then Pablo said with a sniff, "Say, what's that funny eggy smell? Is that your hair? You really do have a thing for those chickens. Dang girl!"

"Well, it's a long story. It's all your fault, ju know. You with that magic stone! I'll tell you all about it over my Tía Lizette's Mexican hot chocolate y los tamales. I'm famished!" I gave Pronto a pat and ran my fingers through his long mane. It felt magical. "Let's go decorate a tree, cowboy!" I gave a *kiss-kiss*. "Let's go, Pronto!"

"Woo-hoo!" Pablo shrieked.

It was a Christmas never to be forgotten, and many more followed for Chicatita and Pablo as their youthful love blossomed over the years. The magic stone eventually went back and stayed with the rest of Pablo's collection from Mexico. And as for María's need for wishes? Well, it turned into a spiritual faith that continued to grow, and she began to see many blessings while embracing each new day as a gift from God.

¡Gracias a Dios!

The Ending For Now

# MAYAN/AZTEC SUN SIGN

DESCRIPTIONS

### Chapter I: Sacrificing Helpful

This day-sign symbolizes personal sacrifice and acceptance of change. It is a sign of politics, practicality, discipline, sacrifice, and organizational skills. Maintaining faith in yourself and staying motivated are issues for you.

### Chapter II: Powerful Charismatic

This sign rules power and charisma as well as emotional upheaval. You are intelligent, adaptable and instinctive, and strong willed. Avoid being an extremist, short tempered, or harsh.

### Chapter III: Authoritative Wise

You are a serious person; a seeker of knowledge with an innate desire to learn as much as you can. You have high standards, are pragmatic and driven to excel in your chosen career. You are status-conscious, wise, with tremendous energy. You are often hardened to life and difficult to reach emotionally. Face life realistically and maintain your personal power.

### Chapter IV: Emotional Imaginative

TOJ represents emotional power and leadership. You are intelligent, sympathetic, humorous, highly versatile, and skilled communicators. You struggle with powerful emotions and urges and can have a tendency to be greedy. You do best when you are generally laid back and take life as it comes.

### Chapter V: Intelligent Secretive

This sign rules psychic abilities and counseling. You are charismatic but secretive and private. You are not afraid of getting involved with other peoples' lives. You have deep faith and are often spiritual or religious and make good healers and consultants. It is important for you to control your aggressions.

### Chapter VI: Careful Useful

This day-sign is easy going by nature, very adaptable, compliant, compromising and helpful. You follow your own tune, work at your own pace, and write your own destiny. You may be slow to get going, but once you start, you don't stop. You have a tendency to hide deep hurts and feelings, and you can be quite moody.

### Chapter VII: Self-Sufficient Romantic

This is a sign of both self-sacrifice and self-interest. You are practical, mechanically inclined, compromising, very social, witty, speak your mind; a mirror of reality. Because self-interest and self-sacrifice can conflict, you have a tendency to be overprotective and to struggle in close relationships.

### Chapter VIII: Knowledgeable Crusading

This sign is associated with knowledge, strong opinions and forcefulness. You are usually popular, accomplished and competent. You have a deep knowledge of human nature, and are good at problem solving and negotiations. You also have tendencies to be intellectually rigid, inflexible, stubborn, opinionated, and prone to argue

### Chapter IX: Thoughtful Conservative

Born under this sign you are deep and introspective. You tend to project an imposing presence, thoughtful, and conservative. Your security needs are very important to you. Daydreaming and fantastic ideas can lead you to insecurity.

### Chapter The Ending: Clever Playful

Rabbit is a sign of cleverness, games and competition. You have an active mind, and you must always be doing something. You have a great liking for music and humor, but you can also be argumentative and even self-destructive at times.

Many thanx to Mayan Majix

You will find an on-line Tzolkin Calculator where you can look up Mayan Sun Signs for free to purchase your own personal pendant, and many other Mayan products.

Visit www.mayanmajix.com

www.ingramcontent.com/pod-product-compliance
Lightning Source LLC
Chambersburg PA
CBHW070820020826
48982CB00014B/33

* 9 7 8 1 6 1 2 4 4 9 4 0 1 *